Book design by Christine Lott

Published by Napoleon Publishing Inc.
Toronto, Ontario, Canada

Canadian Cataloguing in Publication Data

McConnell, G. Robert
    The strawberry jam

ISBN 0-929141-02-4

1. Children's poetry, Canadian (English).*
I. Lott, Christine, 1952- . II. Title

PS8575.C65S7 1990   jC811'.54   C90-094413-7
PZ8.3.M33St 1990

Printed in Canada

The Strawberry Jam

Story by
Robert McConnell

Illustrations by
Christine Lott

The Dark Prince

The Strawberry planet was silent
As the sun began to sink,
And the Strawberry Queen was all alone
To brood and worry and think.

She slouched upon her strawberry throne,
She held her head in her hand;
There was nothing anyone now could do
To save her Strawberry Land.

The halls of the castle were empty,
With everyone locked in their room,
The words that were frozen on their lips
Were death, destruction and doom.

The terrible name of Fraise
Cut through their souls like ice;
It sent a shiver up each spine
And gripped each heart in a vise.

The mind of the Queen was also on Fraise,
On the dark and deadly Prince,
And the thought that he was her nephew
Made her shiver and shudder and wince.

After the death of his parents
She had raised him as her own,
But he had chosen the path of evil
And turned vicious as he'd grown.

And now he was master of Heinous Hall
On the planet's darker side,
And to reach this position of power
He'd stolen, cheated and lied.

For Fraise this was just the beginning,
And he'd sell his soul to Hell,
To finally enslave the Strawberry world
And the Strawberry Queen as well.

He'd plotted and planned with Shortcake,
His twisted, gnome-like friend,
On ways and means and strategies
To reach his evil end.

He'd been training his army of Noshers,
With their insect bodies and claws,
To devastate the strawberry fields
With their razor-like teeth and jaws.

When he sent them out at sunset
They'd obey his every command,
To cut and shred and tear and destroy
The wealth of the Strawberry Land.

Without the strawberry harvest
The planet couldn't survive,
And the Queen would have to surrender
To keep her subjects alive.

The Noshers swept past the castle
In a slashing, slicing stream,
And they gladly did their dirty work
To get their ration of cream.

Cream was all they'd ever eaten,
It was all they'd ever known,
It was all that Fraise had fed them
Since they'd hatched until they'd grown.

Cream was all they wanted,
It was all the Noshers craved,
And cream was what Fraise used
To keep them all enslaved.

They had destroyed the castle gardens
And the land for miles around;
In the place of strawberry fields
There was barren, desolate ground.

And this was but a warning
Of the chilling fate in store —
Unless the Queen surrendered
Her world would be no more.

She thought of her loyal subjects
Who had no safe place to flee,
And she thought of her own dear children,
Young Sillabub and sweet Sillabee.

So she wrote a message to Fraise
With a heavy heart and mind,
The Strawberry throne was his to have —
Her hand trembled as she signed.

Fraise read this painful message
With such foul and fiendish glee,
For he loathed and hated the Queen
And Sillabub and Sillabee.

He sent her clear instructions,
And stressed one terrible thing,
He would soon arrive at the castle
To be greeted as their king.

In exactly seven days
He'd come to claim his throne,
And he expected the greatest welcome
A king was ever shown.

Helpless, hopeless despair and dismay
Swept through the land like waves;
The people had but one short week
Before they all were slaves.

There was nothing they could do
But accept their terrible fate;
They were locked in the grip of evil
And now it was far too late.

Fragola

It was midnight in the castle,
The Queen was all alone;
Tomorrow Fraise would arrive
To claim his long-sought throne.

As the Queen stared into the fire
In empty, cold despair
She had the strangest feeling
That someone else was there.

Out of the flickering shadows
Slipped a wispy, female frame.
The Queen was so utterly shocked
She could barely breathe her name.

"Fragola!" she gasped in awe,
"Is it possible that it's you?
  After all these many years
  I can't believe it's true!

"The day my father died
  You vanished with no trace,
  It was rumored you sought solace
  In a far and distant place."

"I sought the wisdom of the wind,"
  Was the whispered, soft reply,
"I've spent these long and lonely years
  In the shadow of a sigh.

"It's because I loved your father
  That I come to you this night.
  I cannot see you bow to Fraise
  While there's still a chance to fight."

"But it's hopeless!" moaned the Queen,
"There's nothing at all to be done,
  Our freedom will have vanished
  With the rays of the rising sun!"

"There's still a chance," smiled Fragola,
"But it's up to you to choose;
  For if you follow my advice
  There isn't a second to lose."

"Please help us!" pleaded the Queen,
"Our fate is in your hand.
  As the oldest and wisest,
  Can you save our Strawberry Land?

"Tell us what you're thinking,
  We'll do anything you say,
  But there are only six short hours
  Before the break of day!"

"Drain the moat!" ordered Fragola
  In a voice of firm command.
"Send a messenger to every farm
  Throughout the Strawberry Land.

"We need every ounce of cream
  Brought to the castle tonight,
  We haven't a minute to lose
  If we want to win this fight!"

Everyone thought she was crazy,
They thought she was raving mad,
But they also knew that Fragola
Was the only hope they had.

Finally, just before sunrise,
The moat was totally dry,
With thousands of cans of cream
Silhouetted against the sky.

"Pour the cream into the moat!
There is no time to stop!
Empty each and every can!
Don't spill a single drop!"

The moat was finally filled
In the rising rays of the sun.
"Quick, into the castle!" urged Fragola,
"This part of the job is done!"

She ordered everyone present
To the top of the castle wall,
And told them not to be afraid
But stand brave and strong and tall.

She gave each a basket of berries
  And placed it at their feet,
"It's a little surprise for Fraise," she smiled,
"When he and I finally meet."

  Just then someone cried aloud,
"This seems like a terrible dream;
  You've given us some strawberries
  And filled the moat with cream.

"You promised you could save us,
 But this is just absurd,
 It's the absolutely craziest
 Plan that we've ever heard.

"We never should have listened!
 You've surely lost your mind!
 To ever have believed you
 We must be really blind!"

But suddenly panic gripped their hearts,
Their words froze on their lips,
They were seized with total terror
From toes to fingertips.

For marching toward the castle,
The picture of pomp and pride,
Was the dark and deadly Fraise
With Shortcake by his side.

And marching right behind,
On their hideous, crunching claws,
Was the gruesome army of Noshers,
Flashing their razor jaws.

Strawberries

Araise stopped right at the moat
And glared up at the Strawberry Queen,
"Lower the drawbridge!" he hissed,
In a voice that was vicious and mean.

"Do as he says!" whispered Fragola,
"Obey his every command;
We have to make him believe
He's the Lord of the Strawberry Land."

"Lower the drawbridge!" ordered the Queen,
A smile frozen on her face.
"Our new King's throne is waiting,"
She added with elegant grace.

Fraise sauntered onto the drawbridge,
With Shortcake by his side,
"Open the gate and let me in —
This castle is mine!" he cried.

As the Queen was about to obey,
With a heart devoid of hope,
Fragola pulled a knife from her sleeve
And cut the drawbridge rope.

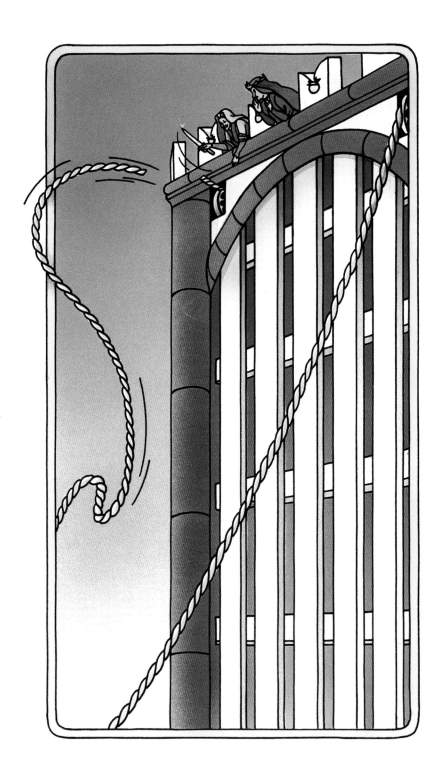

Fraise and little Shortcake
Plunged straight into the cream,
And when they hit that liquid
They both began to scream.

"Help us! Save us! We can't swim!"
They thrashed and churned about,
They yelled to their army of Noshers
To hurry and get them out.

They flailed their arms so wildly,
They twisted, turned and flipped,
That when the Noshers pulled them out
All the cream was whipped.

They were totally covered in cream,
From each toe right to their head,
And forgot in their angry fury
That the Noshers hadn't been fed.

"Get this off us!" Fraise bellowed,
  His hands upon his hips,
  And the Noshers sprang into action
  As they licked their hungry lips.

They went into a frantic frenzy
  Over Fraise and Shortcake dipped,
  For though they had cream every day,
  They'd never had it whipped.

It was at that very moment,
As up to the tower she ran,
That Fragola put into action
The last part of her plan.

"It's strawberry time!" she shouted,
And to show what she had in mind,
She dumped a basket on Fraise and his friend
Of the juiciest she could find.

Everyone soon was doing the same,
Though it all seemed quite insane,
And on Fraise and creamy Shortcake
The strawberries fell like rain.

When the Noshers tasted the berries,
With all the cream on top,
They went totally berserk
And simply couldn't stop.

They devoured every berry,
On Fraise and Shortcake too,
They gobbled up the cream
And even part of a shoe.

And when they'd eaten the berries,
And there simply were no more,
It looked like Fraise and Shortcake
Had just been through a war.

They were bowed and battered and bruised,
And their clothing was in shreds,
They looked absolutely miserable
From their toes right to their heads.

"Attack the castle!" Fraise commanded,
"Destroy everyone inside!
 How dare they do this to their King!
 I'll kill them all!" he cried.

But the Noshers didn't listen
To this furious, wild command;
Their eyes were fixed on Fragola
And the basket in her hand.

She spoke from the top of the tower,
With strawberries in her hair,
And every Nosher stared in awe
As her words rang through the air.

"Leave your evil ways," she said,
"Let me make you understand,
  That we all should work together
  For the good of the Strawberry Land.

"Fraise has taught you to destroy,
  He's taught you only hate,
  But there are good things you could do,
  I know it's not too late.

"You can use your powerful jaws
  To work in the strawberry field,
  And cut and prune the delicate plants
  To double the strawberry yield.

"The Strawberry world will prosper
 If we'll only help each other,
 If we think of people as our friends
 And treat them as a brother.

"In payment for your services
 There'll be a daily Nosher treat,
 Gallons and gallons of fresh whipped cream
 And all the berries you can eat.

"In fact," continued Fragola,
 As she touched her delicate throat,
"If you decide to accept my offer
 You can start by eating the moat.

"But first come into the castle,"
  Urged Fragola the Wise,
"For if you'd like to join us
  There's a very special surprise."

The Noshers didn't hesitate,
Each marched right through the gate,
And soon was seated in a hall
Behind a gleaming plate.

Sillabub and Sillabee,
With Fragola and the Queen,
Served the Noshers endless portions
Of berries and whipped cream.

Meanwhile, Fraise and Shortcake,
Tattered, bruised and broken,
Hobbled off into the distance
And not a word was spoken.

But in their silent fury,
Now that they didn't win,
Each one was blaming the other
For the sorry mess they were in.

The Strawberry planet prospered,
As it never had before.
The Noshers honed their gardening skills
And loved each and every chore.

Fragola stayed at the castle
As closest counsellor to the Queen,
And as the wisest lady in the land
Her power was felt but seldom seen.

Young Sillabub and sweet Sillabee
Grew straight and fair and tall
And helped with the strawberry harvest
When summer turned to fall.

And what of Fraise and Shortcake?
What happened to those two?
I've heard some funny stories
And I'm assuming that they're true.

It seems they returned to Heinous Hall,
Which has fallen into ruin,
And they tend a miserable strawberry patch
By the light of the summer moon.

And they've never forgiven each other
For their pitiful, horrible state;
They loathe everything around them
And their hearts are filled with hate.

Their dream is to conquer the Strawberry world,
But neither can do it alone,
And so they have a little problem
That's no one's fault but their own.

They're both so viciously stubborn,
If you believe what people say,
They haven't spoken a word to each other
Right up to this very day.

It's hate that divides and love that unites,
It will always be that way,
It takes caring and sharing and giving
To turn darkness into day.

The End